RACING THROUGH HISTORY

STOCK CARS
THEN TO NOW

JANEY LEVY

HIGH
interest
books

Children's Press®
A Division of Scholastic Inc.
New York / Toronto / London / Auckland / Sydney
Mexico City / New Delhi / Hong Kong
Danbury, Connecticut

Book Design: Michelle Innes
Contributing Editor: Karl Bollers

Photo Credits: Cover, p. 16 © George Tiedemann/Newsport/Corbis; p. 4 © Lisa
Blumenfeld/Corbis; pp. 8, 10, 14, 21 © Bettmann/Corbis; p. 23 © Getty Images for
NASCAR; p. 24 © Craig Jones/Getty Images; p. 28 © David Taylor/Allsport; p. 30 ©
Ronald Martinez/Getty Images; p. 32 © Robert Laberge/Getty Images; p. 36 © Rusty
Jarett/Getty Images

Library of Congress Cataloging-in-Publication Data

Levy, Janey.
    Racing through history : stock cars then to now / Janey Levy.
    p. cm. — (Stock car racing)
    Includes index.
    ISBN-10: 0-531-16808-5 (lib. bdg.)   0-531-18716-0 (pbk.)
    ISBN-13: 978-0-531-16808-0 (lib. bdg.)   978-0-531-18716-6 (pbk.)
    1. Stock car racing—United States—History—Juvenile literature. I. Title. II.
Series: Stock car racing (Children's Press)

GV1029.9.S74L48 2007
796.720973—dc22
                                                    2006011895

3 4 5 6 7 8 9 10 R 11 10 09 08   62

TABLE OF CONTENTS

The green flag waves stock cars across the starting line as the Nextel Cup Series SUBWAY Fresh 500 kicks off.

INTRODUCTION

Y ou're sitting in your race car, waiting for the green flag to signal the start of the race. This is the first NASCAR race of the season. Nearly 170,000 screaming fans fill the stands. Millions more are watching the race on television. There are over forty cars in the race, and you're near the back of the group. You know you don't stand a chance at winning, but it doesn't matter. This is Daytona Beach, one of the most famous and exciting racetracks in the world and one of NASCAR's great superspeedways.

Racing here is a dream come true. You've wanted to do this ever since you were a kid. Drivers reach speeds of more than 200 miles (322 kilometers) per hour on this track, but that's only one part of Daytona Beach's rich history. Stock car racing has been going on here for seventy years and this is where NASCAR was born. For you, being part of that tradition is an incredible thrill. The green flag waves and the race begins! You're off on the ride of a lifetime!

CHAPTER ONE

THE BEGINNINGS

Fast cars came to Daytona Beach, Florida, in 1902. That's the year world-record automotive speed trials were first held on the sands between Daytona Beach and neighboring Ormond Beach. The fastest drivers from the United States and Europe brought their race cars here to set new speed records. In 1902, the top speed reached at Daytona Beach was 57 miles (92 km) per hour. A top speed of 105 miles (169 km) per hour was reached three years later.

After 1935, the speed trials moved to Utah. Daytona Beach officials decided to replace them with a race. This race would be for stock cars—sedans like the ones ordinary people drive every day. A sedan is an enclosed car for four or more people. The racetrack was created using part of the beach and a highway that ran next to it.

The first Daytona Beach stock car race took place in 1936. It was a financial disaster. The one in 1937 wasn't much better. It was only after two local businessmen took charge in 1938 that the race became a success. A restaurant owner named Charlie Reese provided the money. A gas station owner named William France, Sr., organized and promoted the race. France, nicknamed "Big Bill," would go on to change the history of stock car racing.

Big Bill France was an auto mechanic who began racing when he was a teenager. He used to borrow the family car and go to a nearby racetrack. Big Bill kept racing on local dirt tracks even after he grew up.

Big Bill and his family moved to Daytona Beach in the fall of 1934. There he took a job with a local car dealer. He kept racing and also began to organize and

Stock cars line up at the start of an amateur auto race at Daytona Beach, Florida back in 1925.

promote races. After the 1938 Daytona Beach stock car race, Big Bill kept thinking about ways to make racing better. He decided to retire from driving and concentrate on improving the sport instead.

In December 1947, Big Bill organized a meeting of car owners, drivers, and mechanics at a Daytona Beach hotel. The purpose of the meeting was to establish standards and rules for stock car racing. The National Association of Stock Car Auto Racing (NASCAR) was created at that meeting. Big Bill was elected as its president.

NASCAR is a sanctioning body. It sets rules for racing and it sanctions, or approves, races that follow the rules. Before NASCAR, different racetracks had different rules. NASCAR established uniform rules and made sure they were enforced. NASCAR also set up a points system. Drivers would earn points in a race based on how well they did. They would also earn points based on how many laps they led during the race. The driver with the most points at the end of the season would be the national champion.

The first NASCAR race took place on February 15, 1948. It was held at Daytona Beach. More than fourteen thousand fans attended the race. Red Byron was the winner.

NASCAR held fifty-two races in 1948. The cars in these races were known as "modifieds." They were stock cars that had been modified to improve their performance. The national champion at the end of the season was the same man who won the first race— Red Byron.

NASCAR introduced the Strictly Stock Series in 1949. This series was for stock cars that hadn't been modified at all. The first race was held at Charlotte, North Carolina, on June 19. More than thirteen thousand fans

Drivers compete to win the endurance record in the 24-hour Continental race at Daytona Beach.

RACING ROOTS

Stock car racing became popular in the southern United States in the 1930s. It started among moonshine runners. These were men who hauled homemade whiskey, known as moonshine, for a living. From 1920 to 1933, alcoholic beverages were illegal in the United States. This period was known as Prohibition. Moonshine runners had to drive fast to outrun the federal agents who were trying to stop them. They souped up their cars to make them go faster and developed the skills needed to drive them. When they weren't hauling moonshine, the runners liked to race each other.

filled the stands. The large attendance told Big Bill that Strictly Stock would be a successful series.

Big Bill changed the name of the Strictly Stock Series in 1950. He thought it needed one that sounded more polished and professional, so he renamed it the Grand National Series. The series expanded and the number of races more than doubled. The number of states where races were held also increased, but the Grand National was still a regional series in spite of its name.

CHAPTER TWO

GROWTH AND CHANGE

The Grand National Series needed a blockbuster event to attract more attention to the sport. It got one on September 4, 1950, when the series held its first 500-mile (800 km) race. It took place at the brand-new Darlington Raceway in Darlington, South Carolina. This was NASCAR's first superspeedway. A superspeedway is a paved racetrack that is at least 1 mile (2 km) long. It was paved at a time when most NASCAR racetracks were still dirt. The race at Darlington was a huge success. It had a twenty-five thousand dollar purse, or prize, which was an enormous amount of money at the time. Seventy-five drivers took part and twenty-five thousand fans attended.

In spite of the race's success, most people still thought of stock car racing as a southern sport, not a national one. In 1956, that began to change. NASCAR began to include more races on paved tracks. It also included more races on road courses, in addition to those on standard oval tracks. Races were held in more parts of the country and another superspeedway was built. This one was at Daytona Beach, NASCAR's birthplace.

Big Bill wanted to build a superspeedway at Daytona Beach ever since he had seen the one at Darlington. He finally succeeded, and Daytona International Speedway opened in 1959. It was just the kind of showplace that NASCAR needed. The first Daytona 500 was held on February 22, 1959. An enormous crowd of forty-one thousand fans attended and they thrilled to an exciting race that ended in a photo finish. A photo finish is a very close race, where a photograph has to be studied to decide which racer has won.

NASCAR's growth and increasing popularity finally won it attention from the national press. On January 31, 1960, NASCAR received its first live television coverage. This was the first television program devoted entirely to stock car racing.

Richard Petty's stock car rolls over after accidentally hitting a retaining wall.

COATTAIL RIDER

A racer named Junior Johnson made a discovery during practice for the 1960 Daytona 500. His car could not go as fast as many other cars there. He found out it went much faster, however, if he got behind a faster car and drove very close to its back bumper. This technique came to be known as drafting. It's been an important technique used in stock car racing ever since.

The Grand National Series continued to grow and change. In 1972, it became the Winston Cup Series. Its popularity led NASCAR to create other racing series. In 1982, NASCAR created a second stock car series called the Busch Series. The Busch Series is the junior series. To this day, the cars are slightly smaller and most of the drivers are less experienced. In 1995, NASCAR created a series for stock trucks called the Craftsman Truck Series. In 2004, the Winston Cup Series became the Nextel Cup Series. All the current series are named for their primary sponsors.

The driver of the Number 17 NTN Bearings Toyota races ahead of the pack at the NASCAR Craftsman Truck Series EasyCare Vehicle Service Contracts 200.

The first live television coverage of a full Winston Cup race occurred in 1979. Beginning in 1989, all Winston Cup races were televised. By the time the Craftsman Truck Series was created, there was a huge national audience for NASCAR races. As a result, there was television coverage for all the Craftsman Truck races during their first full season.

16

There's no end in sight to the growing popularity of NASCAR. Millions of people have discovered the excitement of stock car racing, but it's not just the racing itself the fans enjoy. The drivers are a big part of NASCAR's popularity and it's been that way since the beginning. Big Bill France knew from the start that fans don't come just to see the race. They come to see the racers.

CHAPTER THREE

LEGENDARY STOCK CAR DRIVERS

Many colorful drivers have been part of stock car racing over the last seventy years. One of them was Red Byron, NASCAR's very first champion. Red was a World War II (1939–1945) hero who was severely wounded when his plane was shot down. He spent more than two years in the hospital. Red's wounds led to problems with his left leg. When he was racing his car, his left shoe had to be bolted to the stock car's clutch pedal because of these problems. In spite of this, Red won the national championship in 1949 and 1950. Unfortunately, his health problems forced him to retire after only three seasons. He died in 1960.

Among other famous early NASCAR racers were the Flock brothers—Bob, Fonty, and Tim. Bob and Fonty were moonshine runners before they became racers. All three brothers raced in the Strictly Stock Series in 1949 and in the Grand National Series in the 1950s. Altogether, the brothers won eighty-three poles and sixty-two races. A pole is the number one starting position in a race. A driver wins the pole position by being the fastest in a qualifying race.

Edward Glenn "Fireball" Roberts is considered one of the best, most popular drivers in NASCAR history. His nickname, however, doesn't have anything to do with his racing. He got it because he was an outstanding baseball pitcher. Fireball's NASCAR career lasted from 1950 to 1964 and he won thirty-five poles and thirty-three races during that time. His career ended tragically when he died in a crash during a race in May 1964.

Another popular and very successful NASCAR driver was Robert Glenn "Junior" Johnson. Like Bob and Fonty Flock, he was a former moonshine runner. Junior was a team owner as well as a driver. His driving career lasted from 1953 through 1966. As a driver, Junior won forty-seven poles and fifty races. Junior became a successful businessman after he retired from racing.

FAST FACT

Fonty Flock was known for his unusual racing clothes. He always wore shorts, black shoes, and black socks. As part of a publicity stunt, Tim Flock raced for a while with a monkey named Jocko Flock in the car with him!

Ned Jarrett was one of NASCAR's most well-respected racers. He was known as "Gentleman Ned" because of his polite manner. Ned's career in the Grand National Series lasted from 1953 through 1966. He won thirty-five poles and fifty races. He won the Grand National championship twice—in 1961 and again in 1965. His son, Dale, has been a NASCAR driver since 1982. Dale won the Winston Cup championship in 1999.

Richard Petty may be the best driver in NASCAR history. He's known as "The King" for all his racing accomplishments. His career lasted from 1958 through 1992. Richard won 127 poles. No other NASCAR driver has won as many. He won two hundred races, setting another NASCAR record. Richard holds the record for the most wins in a season and for the most wins in a row. He won the Daytona 500 seven times—also a record. Richard belongs to a NASCAR racing family. His father, Lee,

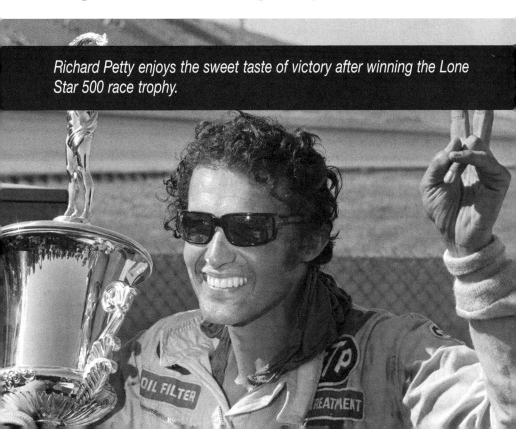

Richard Petty enjoys the sweet taste of victory after winning the Lone Star 500 race trophy.

won the Winston Cup championship in 1954, 1958, and 1959. His son, Kyle, began racing in the Winston Cup Series in 1979.

Wendell Scott holds a unique place in NASCAR history. He was the first African American NASCAR driver. Like Bob and Fonty Flock and Junior Johnson, he was a moonshine runner before he was a racer. His NASCAR career lasted from 1961 through 1973. Wendell had to fight against racism during his entire

HORSEPOWER MEETS GIRL POWER

Three women raced in the early days of NASCAR: Sara Christian, Ethel Mobley, and Louise Smith. Sara was the first woman to drive in a NASCAR race. Ethel was the sister of the Flock brothers. She beat all her brothers in one Grand National race. Louise had never even seen a race before she raced in her first one. She placed third in that race and kept driving even after the race had ended! No one told her that the checkered flag meant it was over. Louise's aggressive driving caused her to crash in many races. She crashed so often that kids came up to her before races to ask if she was going to crash.

career. He had trouble getting sponsors and people tried to sabotage his race car. He kept on in spite of the problems and won one race in 1963. At first, because of the color of his skin, he wasn't awarded the victory. The trophy was given to a white driver instead. NASCAR officials feared riots would break out among white southerners if an African American won. After Wendell complained, he was quietly awarded his victory a few days later. He was given a cheap, wooden trophy that didn't have his name (or

Wendell Scott mentors young driver Joe Henderson III before a try-out at South Boston Speedway.

why he had received it) on it. The 1977 movie *Greased Lightning* is based on his life.

Another great NASCAR driver was Dale Earnhardt. He was known as "The Intimidator" because of his aggressive driving style. His Winston Cup career lasted from 1975 to 2001. Dale won twenty-two poles and seventy-six races. He's the only driver besides Richard Petty to win seven championships. Dale came from a NASCAR racing family. His father, Ralph, was a Winston Cup racer. His son, Dale, Jr., began racing in the

Dale Earnhardt, Jr. poses for a photo opportunity with his late father, racing legend Dale Earnhardt, Sr.

Winston Cup Series in 2000 and is one of the top NASCAR drivers today. Dale Earnhardt's career ended tragically in 2001. He died in an accident during the Daytona 500.

These drivers all helped to make stock car racing the immensely popular sport it is today. The talented, young drivers who are currently part of NASCAR's top racing series are also contributing. One such driver is Jeff Gordon. Jeff has won the championship four times. Kurt Busch, who won the championship in 2004, is another. Tony Stewart is a rising star who won the championship in 2002 and 2005. Fresh faces join the Nextel Cup Series every year. Some of them will be the racing legends of the future.

FAST FACT

The part of Wendell Scott in the 1977 movie **Greased Lightning** was played by famous comedian and actor Richard Pryor. The advertising campaign featured the tagline, "Richard Pryor Drives 'Em Wild!"

CHAPTER FOUR

HOW SPONSORS MAKE A DIFFERENCE

Big money helps keep NASCAR moving. It takes millions of dollars just to own a race car or a team. In addition to this, many drivers can earn millions each year. This wasn't always the case. Stock car racers earned very little in the early days. Red Byron, the 1949 Strictly Stock champion, won only

$5,800 that year. A big reason for the change has been the role played by sponsors. Sponsors provide money to support teams and for prizes. Sponsors have been around since the early days, but their role has grown dramatically over the years. So has the amount of money they put into racing. As NASCAR's popularity grew, the types of sponsors changed.

In the beginning, sponsors were often local. The first major national sponsor was the Mercury Outboard Motor Company, which made boat motors. Carl Kiekhaefer was the company owner. In 1955 and 1956, Carl owned several race cars in the Grand National Series. He put his company name on his race cars and put a lot of money into maintaining and improving his vehicles. His cars won a lot of races. In fact, Tim Flock was driving for Carl when he won the Grand National championship in 1955. Sales of Carl's boat motors increased. People in racing quickly learned what a difference a sponsor could make. At the same time, people in business learned about the benefits of sponsoring race cars.

Carl didn't stay involved in NASCAR for long, but his success encouraged other major companies to become sponsors. Most of these companies were more

NASCAR owes much of its success to the contributions that many different sponsors have made over the years.

directly involved with cars. Some of them manufactured cars while others made parts and supplies. That changed dramatically in the early 1970s.

NASCAR had grown a lot since 1949 and was still growing. Costs were also increasing. Teams needed more money from sponsors to keep operating, but they were receiving less.

In 1970, Junior Johnson took a big step when he decided to ask the R. J. Reynolds Tobacco Company to sponsor his team. Television advertising of tobacco products had just become illegal. He knew that Reynolds had advertising money to spend and needed to find a new way to spend it.

Junior thought Reynolds might be interested in putting some of that money into a race team. Better than that, Reynolds made the decision to sponsor the entire Grand National Series! Reynolds put so much money into the

FAST FACT

Carl Kiekhaefer originally wrote "Mercury Outboards" on his race cars to advertise his boat-motor company. He later found out people thought he was advertising Mercury automobiles, so he changed the writing to "Kiekhaefer Outboards."

series that NASCAR decided to change its name. That's why the Grand National Series became the Winston Cup Series in 1972.

The money that Reynolds put into NASCAR gave it the power to affect the very nature of the series. Reynolds suggested that NASCAR reduce the number of races from about fifty to about thirty per year and it did. The races it dropped were at small tracks. These tracks had been important to the growth of stock car racing, but they

The drivers are neck and neck during the NASCAR Busch Series O'Reilly 300 at the Texas Motor Speedway.

weren't part of NASCAR anymore.

Being a NASCAR sponsor proved to be a smart way for Reynolds to market its products. This encouraged many other major companies that had nothing to do with cars to become NASCAR sponsors. That trend continues today.

Reynolds put hundreds of millions of dollars into NASCAR racing over a period of thirty years. In later years, Reynolds felt much pressure because of government legislation aimed at curbing cigarette

advertising. In 2002, the company decided to end its sponsorship of the Winston Cup Series. Nextel, one of the largest telecommunications companies in the world, announced that it would become the new sponsor. Once again, NASCAR renamed the series in honor of its new sponsor and the Winston Cup Series became the Nextel Cup Series in 2004.

Like Reynolds before it, Nextel spends huge amounts of money as a sponsor. Individual team sponsors also

spend a lot of money. A sponsor may spend ten to twenty million dollars a year on a team. This money helps the teams and NASCAR to grow, but they're not the only ones that benefit.

The companies are willing to spend the money because it's good advertising for their brand. The sponsor's name goes on the race car and the uniforms worn by the driver and the pit crew. It also goes on the trucks that transport the car and equipment. In addition, the sponsor gets to use the driver in advertisements for their products.

The sponsor chooses the colors used for the cars and the team uniforms. The sponsor even has a say in what drivers the team hires. Some might wonder if it's good for sponsors to wield as much power as they do, but one thing is certain—NASCAR wouldn't have become as successful as it is without their support.

Pit crews are able to change stock car tires in just a matter of seconds.

CHAPTER FIVE

WHAT'S NEXT?

NASCAR hasn't finished growing and changing. In January 2006, NASCAR announced that the Car of Tomorrow will be used in Nextel Cup races beginning in 2007. The Car of Tomorrow is specifically designed to improve safety and competition. It is larger, which will protect the driver better in case of impact. It is also less sleek than current stock cars.

The results are slower, safer vehicles. These cars will be used in sixteen Nextel Cup races in 2007 and in all Nextel Cup races beginning in 2009.

NASCAR has also begun to attract foreign car manufacturers. In the early days of NASCAR, there were a few foreign cars in its races, but there haven't been any since 1958. However, after enforcing a decades-long rule that only allowed competition among cars made by American automobile companies, NASCAR revised it to include cars assembled in the United States. This meant foreign cars could compete as long as they were built on American soil.

Toyota currently has a plant in Georgetown, Kentucky, and already has trucks running in NASCAR's Craftsman Truck Series. It will begin running cars in the Busch and Nextel Cup Series in 2007. If Toyota has success with its cars, other foreign car manufacturers may also become interested in NASCAR.

NASCAR continues to add new venues, or places where it holds races. NASCAR's popularity is growing in the western United States. As a result, NASCAR added new races in Texas, Arizona, and California in 2005. NASCAR is even beginning to spread outside the United States. NASCAR Mexico was established in 2004. A

Bret Bodine and Kyle Petty test-drive two different versions of NASCAR's Car of Tomorrow at the Daytona International Speedway.

Busch Series race was held in Mexico for the first time in 2005. This race is now a regular part of the Busch Series.

NASCAR Canada was also established in 2004. NASCAR already has many Canadian fans and NASCAR Canada will provide them with more information about the sport they love. It will also increase television coverage of NASCAR events in Canada.

In addition, NASCAR is actively trying to increase the number of women and minorities in stock car racing. There have been women and minorities in stock car racing over the years, but from the beginning most of the drivers and crew members have been white males. NASCAR wants to change that. Since 2004, it has had a special program whose goal is to help talented young women and minorities gain more experience.

Stock car racing has come a long way from the races on the sand at Daytona Beach. Today, it is the second most popular spectator sport in the United States. Only professional football is more popular. That may change as NASCAR continues to grow.

NASCAR's Craftsman Truck Series brings a lot of new enthusiasm and excitement to the world of racing.

STOCK CAR FIRSTS

First NASCAR race
Daytona Beach, FL, February 15, 1948

First NASCAR Strictly Stock champion
Red Byron, 1949

First woman to run a NASCAR race
Sara Christian, Charlotte Motor Speedway, NC,
June 19, 1949

First NASCAR superspeedway
Darlington Raceway, SC, 1950

First Grand National race held west of the Mississippi River
Carrell Speedway, Gardena, CA, April 8, 1951

First NASCAR team owner to use major sponsors
Carl Kiekhaefer, 1955

First race car driver to be named Professional Athlete of the Year by the Florida Sports Writers Association
Edward Glenn "Fireball" Roberts, 1958

First live television broadcast of a NASCAR event
Qualifying races from Daytona International Speedway,
Daytona, FL, January 31, 1960, on CBS Broadcasting

First use of two-way radio communication in a NASCAR race
Firecracker 250 at Daytona International Speedway,
Daytona, FL, July 4, 1960

First African American driver to win a Grand National race
Wendell Scott, Jacksonville Speedway Park, FL,
December 1, 1963

First NASCAR driver to go faster than 200 miles (322 km) per hour
Buddy Baker, in a test run at Talladega Superspeedway,
AL, March 24, 1970

First woman to qualify for the Daytona 500
Janet Guthrie, Daytona, FL, February 20, 1977

First live television coverage of a complete NASCAR race
Daytona 500, Daytona, FL, February 18, 1979

First NASCAR driver to go faster than 200 miles (322 km) per hour in an official qualifying lap
Benny Parsons, Talladega Superspeedway, AL,
April 29, 1982

First year every NASCAR Winston Cup race shown on television
1989

First woman voted into the International Motorsports Hall of Fame
Louise Smith, 1999

NEW WORDS

automotive (aw-tuh-mo-tiv) relating to self-propelled vehicles or machines

checkered flag (chek-urd flag) the black-and-white checkered flag that signals the end of the race; it is waved as the winner crosses the finish line

coverage (kuhv-ur-ij) news as presented by reporters for newspapers, radio, and television

minority (muh-nor-uh-tee) a group of people of a particular race, ethnic group, or religion living among a larger group of a different race, ethnic group, or religion

moonshine (moon-shine) homemade whiskey

pole (pohl) the number-one starting position in a race; a driver wins the pole position by being the fastest in qualifying

Prohibition (pro-hi-bish-en) period from 1920 to 1933 when alcoholic beverages were illegal in the United States

purse (purss) the total amount of money offered as prizes for a race

qualifying race (kwahl-uh-fye-ing rayss) the method for determining where each driver lines up to start a race

road course (rohd korss) a racetrack that has twists and turns like a road

NEW WORDS

sabotage (sab-uh-tahzh) deliberate damage or destruction

sanctioning body (sangk-shuhn-ing bod-ee) an organization that has the authority to set rules and approve events for a sport

sedan (si-dan) an enclosed car for four or more people

soup up (soop uhp) to increase power to an engine or motor vehicle

sponsor (spon-sur) a person or company that helps pay the cost of a racing event or a race team in return for advertising rights

stock car (stok kar) a race car built to look like an ordinary car

superspeedway (soo-pur-speed-way) a paved racetrack that is at least 1 mile (2 km) long

telecommunications (tel-uh-kuh-myoo-nuh-kay-shuhnz) science that deals with the sending of messages over long distances by telephone, satellite, radio, or other electronic means

televise (tel-uh-vize) to broadcast on television

venue (ven-yoo) a place where an event is held

FOR FURTHER READING

Buckley, James. *NASCAR*. New York: DK Children's Publishing, 2005.

Golenbock, Peter, Seiji Ogata, and Greg Fielden, eds. *NASCAR Encyclopedia*. St. Paul, MN: Motorbooks International Publishing Company, 2003.

Kelley, K. C., and Bob Woods. *Young Stars of NASCAR*. Pleasantville, NY: Reader's Digest Children's Publishing, 2006.

Sporting News Books. *NASCAR Record & Fact Book: 2006 Edition*. St. Louis, MO: The Sporting News, 2006.

Woods, Bob. *The Greatest Races*. Pleasantville, NY: Reader's Digest Children's Publishing, 2004.

RESOURCES

ORGANIZATIONS

International Motorsports Hall of Fame
P.O. Box 1018
Talladega, AL 35161
Phone: (256) 362-5002
http://www.motorsportshalloffame.com

**Joe Weatherly Stock Car Museum and National
Motorsports Press Association Hall of Fame**
1301 Harry Byrd Highway
P.O. Box 500
Darlington, SC 29532
Phone: (866) 459-7223
http://www.darlingtonraceway.com/track%5Finfo/museum

**National Association for Stock Car Auto Racing
(NASCAR)**
P.O. Box 2875
Daytona Beach, FL 32120
Phone: (386) 253-0611
http://www.nascar.com

RESOURCES

WEB SITES

Darlington Raceway
http://www.darlingtonraceway.com
The official site of NASCAR's first superspeedway sells tickets to racing events, covers breaking news, and has an online store.

Daytona International Speedway
http://www.daytonainternationalspeedway.com
This cool Web site sells tickets to racing events, offers news coverage about the world of stock car racing, and has an online store.

International Motorsports Hall of Fame
http://www.motorsportshalloffame.com
This site offers a virtual tour, lists a who's who of famous stock car racers, and has its own hall of fame photo gallery.

NASCAR
http://www.nascar.com
This official racing site includes news, schedules, and information on racing teams as well as on individual drivers.

INDEX

A
automotive, 6

B
Byron, Red, 9-10, 18-19, 26, 40

C
Charlotte, 10, 40
checkered flag, 22
coverage, 14, 16, 38, 41
Craftsman Truck Series, 15-16, 35, 39

D
Darlington Raceway, 12-13, 40
Daytona Beach, 5-7, 9-10, 13, 15, 21, 25, 37-38, 40

E
Earnhardt, Dale, 24-25

F
Flock brothers, 19-20, 22, 27
France, William "Big Bill," 7, 17

G
Grand National Series, 11-12, 15, 19-20, 22, 27, 30, 40-41
green flag, 4-5

J
Jarrett, Ned, 20
Johnson, Junior, 15, 22, 29

M
mechanic, 7, 9
minorities, 38
moonshine, 11, 19-20, 22

N
NASCAR, 5, 9-10, 13-35, 37-41
Nextel Cup Series, 4, 15, 25, 32, 34-35

P
Petty, Richard, 14, 21
pole, 19-21, 24
Prohibition, 11
purse, 13

INDEX

ABOUT THE AUTHOR

Janey Levy is a writer and editor who lives in Colden, New York. She is the author of more than fifty books for young people.